Badger the Mystical Mutt

A round of "up-paws" for *Badger the Mystical Mutt*

"Set to be the Top Dog of children's books ... a magical debut of a book." Social Literary

"Kids' book takes world by storm." The Scottish Sun

"A moving and joyful story which warmed the heart of this cynical old journalist." That's Books

"First-time winner." The Evening Times

"A toast-loving, magical hound, who has been winning fans in book shops, libraries and schools across Scotland." The List

"A charming and very funny children's story." Diana Cooper

"McNicol & Jackson have created a charming new book character; a toast-crunching hound named Badger."
Aye Write, Glasgow's Book Festival

"A truly magical story which has all the hallmarks of a future children's classic!" Ursula James

"A magical 21st-century narrative which will delight and inspire folk of all ages."
Alex Lewczuk, Southside Broadcasting

"The toast-crunching, spell-muffing Badger the Mystical Mutt is a delightful, madcap, magical character, who worms his way into your affections." Maggie Woods, MotorBar

Badger the Mystical Mutt

McNicol & Jackson

THE LUNICORN PRESS

THE LUNICORN PRESS
Glasgow

First published 2011 by The Lunicorn Press.
Reprinted 2012 and 2013
5

Printed by Martins the Printers, Berwick-upon-Tweed
Designed and typeset by Taras Young
Set in 14.25pt Gentium Book

British Library Cataloguing in Publication Data
A CIP catalogue record for this book is available from the British Library

ISBN 978-0-9569640-0-7

www.badgerthemysticalmutt.com
www.facebook.com/badgermutt
www.twitter.com/badgermutt

For Rosemary Boiteux

Also by McNicol and Jackson

Badger the Mystical Mutt and the Barking Boogie

Chapter One

It was a quarter past midsummer. In a garden, next to a lane, Badger the Mystical Mutt was feeling rather pleased with himself.

At last, he had gathered all the ingredients for his fabulous new spell to conjure up his favourite treat — a higgledy-piggledy tower of toast.

"This is great," he thought smugly.

Sparkles of light appeared around his tail. Badger bounced around in a circle and shimmied his bottom.

"*Buttercups and sun scorched grass,*
Do for me this easy task.
Take this bread and make it roast.

Turn it into buttered toast," whispered Badger and closed his eyes.

He waited. All was quiet.

Too quiet.

Then, Boom! Crack! Bang!

"Oops!" said Badger, feeling his eyebrows smoulder. He opened one eye nervously to see a pile of burnt crumbs in front of him.

"Not quite as I'd planned. I need to practise that one. Time for a lie down."

Badger fell quickly into a deep sleep and dreamt of hot toast dripping with butter.

Suddenly, a breeze lifted a scrunched up ball of paper and dropped it squarely on Badger's nose. He jumped from his slumber and shook his head. A tattered old newspaper lay on the grass beside him.

Badger sighed and smoothed out the newspaper with his large paws. The Big Folk would get the news a lot faster if they used pee-mail, he thought. A lift of the leg on a lamppost and the neighbourhood knew everything, smiled Badger to himself.

He peered at the pages.

That's Hamish, he thought, as he spied a large picture of a floppy-eared spaniel with the headline: 'Local mutt favourite to win *Pet Idol* contest'. And there's Top Dog and his gang, he frowned, spotting a large 'Wanted' poster on the opposite page.

Top Dog would not be happy. He and his gang had been fleeing the Dog Catcher for a long time. I smell trouble ahead, thought Badger.

Meanwhile, in the lane at the bottom of the garden, all was not well. Hamish was running for his life. Hot on his heels was Top Dog, leader of the lane and all-round bruiser. Hurtling along behind him was his ferocious gang of five: Pogo Paws, Pickle, Dodgy Dave, Snif and Lennie.

Hamish raced like he never had before. He passed ladders and old paint tins, dodged bicycle bits, brushes and shovels and ploughed through messy piles of freshly mown grass.

He could hear the gang getting closer and closer. His heart pounded and his chest heaved. He had to do something to slow them down.

Up ahead, he spotted a crate of rotting fruit. That might stop them in their tracks, he thought.

He sprinted faster towards the crate and threw his whole weight against it. It tilted and toppled behind him. Squidgy oranges, apples and bananas littered the lane. Hamish drew breath. The gang fell flat on their backs and thrashed angrily on the ground.

"Pooperscoopersmellysnooper," yelled Top Dog pointing at the *Wanted* poster on the lamp post. "Thanks to you and your *Pet Idol* rubbish, the Dog Catcher is on the prowl. The competition is coming to town, so he wants to round up all the strays."

"We'll make sure you *never* win *Pet Idol,*" snarled Snif.

"Fancy Pants thinks he's a Smarty Pants now," growled Dodgy Dave.

"Get him!" they screamed, scrambling to their paws.

Uh oh, thought Hamish. Here we go again.

He took off at speed, heading this time for a pile of silver bins at the far end of the lane.

There's nothing else for it, he winced, but a full-on collision.

Hamish dived at the bins, sending them flying. As they clattered and clanged, bumped and banged, the gang scattered.

All was quiet.

Hamish found himself flat on the floor under a big, black lid.

I feel like a turtle, he thought to himself.

Hamish picked himself up and crawled tentatively onwards with his bin-lid shell.

This is an amazing disguise, he thought, but it's a bit dark. He tripped and came face to face with a big wooden fence.

Top Dog and his gang were nowhere to be seen.

"Phew!" Hamish breathed a sigh of relief as, looking round, he spotted a gaping crack in the fence. He shook off the bin lid and put it down carefully.

Now *that*, thought Hamish, feeling pleased with himself, could be a useful hiding place for any more scuffles with Top Dog and his gang.

He peered through the crack and spied a big black lump of snoring fur.

Is that Badger the Mystical Mutt? wondered Hamish.

He narrowed his eyes and caught sight of Badger's famous red-spotted neckerchief.

It was him! Some said you could see sparkles of light around him and that he was quite, quite magical. And others said he saw things *differently*.

Badger scratched his head with his paw, his nose twitched and he sniffed the air around him. Then he trotted to the garden fence, jumped on to his hind legs and peered into next door's garden, staring hard at whatever was on the other side of the fence.

His ears pointed forward and sparkles of light appeared around his big rubbery nose. Just then a freshly baked smell wafted towards Hamish and he saw a pile of toast float over the fence.

"I'm still working on that landing," said Badger to the toast, as it nose-dived sharply to the ground.

"Fetch!" said Badger to no one in particular.

Suddenly, Badger's neckerchief unravelled and shot across the garden, scooped up the toast and dropped it into Badger's bowl.

"Nice one, 'Chief," said Badger.

The neckerchief swirled around, opened out, covered the top of Badger's head in a pretty headscarf and tied itself in a knot under his chin.

"Not quite as I'd planned," said Badger, "but thanks for the toast."

"Supersnackaroony!" shouted an excited Hamish, giggling. "Now I know why the others call you *magical.*"

Badger looked around sharply, startled by the voice behind the crack in the fence, and more than a little embarrassed.

Just then, Hamish heard the sound of heavy paws beating their way towards him. Top Dog and his gang were back on his tail.

Chapter Two

Hamish stumbled quickly through the fence, tripped and landed at Badger's feet with a thump.

Badger lifted his head and sighed.

Hamish shifted from paw to paw.

"What's the matter, Hamish?" asked Badger, noticing that Hamish's long floppy ears were tied together in a knot on top of his head. "What happened to your ears?"

Hamish looked up, trying to see his re-arranged ears.

"Oh, that? It's nothing really. I just have to walk past them and they …"

Badger interrupted. "Let me guess! Top

Dog and his gang?"

Hamish nodded woefully.

"I don't know what I've done. I just mind my own business and they still pick on me. They keep calling me Fancy Pants and shouted something about *Pet Idol.*"

"Ah yes," said Badger. "I picked up the pee-mail about that and saw it in the Big Folk's newspaper. You're favourite to win, Hamish."

"But I don't know anything about it," said Hamish wearily.

"The Dog Catcher has put an advertisement in the paper and posters on the lamp posts about Top Dog and his gang," sighed Badger.

"What's that got to do with *Pet Idol*?"

"Because you've been nominated in the contest, the lane is in the spotlight."

"But why is that my fault?" asked Hamish, a bit baffled.

"I don't know. Why don't I show you some tricks to make you smile so you can forget about *Pet Idol* for a while?" said Badger. "Watch this."

"Okay," sighed Hamish. "Is this why they call you Badger the Mystical Mutt?"

"Well Hamish, Badger the Mystical Mutt was a name given to me by my ancestors. I have travelled the world for centuries, and now I have ended up in this garden with these Big Folk to carry on using magical powers for good."

"Er ... right!" said Hamish.

"See this tail?"

Hamish examined his long-haired, sleek, swishing tail.

"This isn't just any tail. It's a Badgical Magical tail. Have you seen those gigantic flying machines in the sky, carrying the Big Folk from one country to another?"

"Erm … well… they're very noisy. They're not birds, are they?"

"No, they're not birds. The Big Folk made them; modelled on my invention, of course. Watch and learn."

Badger straightened his legs and wagged his bottom until his tail began to whirr. Within seconds, Badger lifted off from the ground and hovered in the air above Hamish.

"Wow!" exclaimed Hamish, as Badger circled him mischievously.

"If I add my famous doggie sky-paddle, I can move forwards and steer in any direction."

Badger's big paws climbed the air in front of him and he rose higher and higher until he was level with his Big Folk's roof.

"Awesome!" squealed Hamish who, by now, was chasing his own tail in excitement.

"But how do you get down?"

"I haven't quite mastered that particular manoeuvre yet," shouted Badger, as his tail stopped whirring, his paws stopped climbing and he plummeted swiftly to the grass with a thud.

"It's still awesome," said Hamish in

complete admiration.

Badger jumped to his feet, shaking himself vigorously. "So, let me see…"

"You mean … there's more?" asked Hamish, who had now forgotten his earlier trauma with Top Dog and was more than a little impressed.

"Of course. See this nose?"

Badger's big brown eyes went cross-eyed as he focused fondly on his snout. Hamish looked on intently and nodded.

"This nose is not just any nose. It's a Badgical Magical nose. Not only can it detect browning bread in toasters next door, but also aromas the length and breadth of the country … and beyond. From a toasted baguette in the French Riviera to a freshly heated poppadom in the Far East; from a large Lancashire loaf to a buttered bagel in New York City. I can sniff them all!"

"Goodness!" said Hamish.

Badger, enjoying the attention, continued:

"Once a famous spy asked for help with a special sniffing mission. Now, even the secret service has adopted these methods to catch out the baddies."

"Goodness!" repeated Hamish, eager for Badger's next tale.

"And last, but by no means least, have you seen the big white plates stuck on the walls of the Big Folk's houses?"

Hamish nodded.

"Naturally, I gave them the specifications for such objects, based on my very own ears," said Badger.

"Why? What are they for, and how are they connected to your ears? Your ears are black and furry and much smaller than those big dishes."

"Ah," said Badger, "like me, they get messages from space." His ears began to revolve and he shouted excitedly, "Sonic boom boom!"

"Wow!" said Hamish

"Not just any ears, Hamish, these are…"

"Badgical magical ears!" shouted Hamish.

"You've got it! And that, my friend, is why I am called Badger the Mystical Mutt. Now, why are you here again?" asked Badger.

Hamish pointed a paw upwards to his long floppy ears, which were still tied in a knot on the top of his head.

"Ah yes. Let's get that sorted."

Badger untied Hamish's ears until they hung properly at the side of his head.

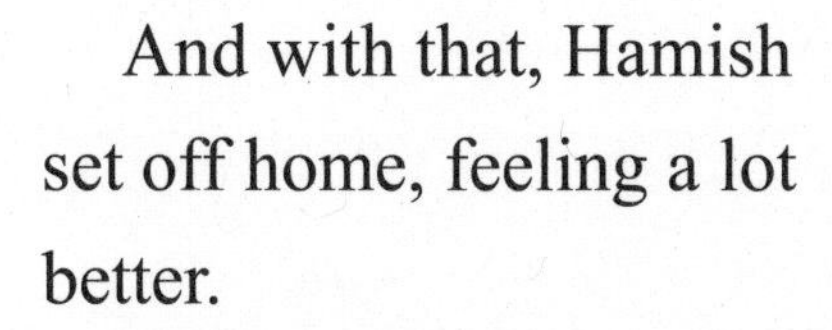

"Now, next time you come face to face with Top Dog and his gang, tell them that they're just jealous because you're in the competition and they're not."

And with that, Hamish set off home, feeling a lot better.

But he had only just stepped back into the lane when he heard a strange click and scraping noise right next to his ears.

He spun round in panic.

"Not so pretty now, Hamish!" snarled Top Dog, waving a pair of gleaming scissors in his face.

Chapter Three

The rest of the gang, who were each armed with their own set of shears, pinned him to the ground as Top Dog held the scissors over his head.

"Let's see if you can win first prize now, Fancy Pants!"

"No!" yelped Hamish. "Please … Don't do that!"

"Too late, Pretty Boy!" scowled Top Dog, cutting some of the hairs from the top of Hamish's head.

The gang gave Hamish a haircut until all he was left with were spiky tufts.

"See you in the final!" said Top Dog, as

he and the rest of his gang ran off, cackling gleefully.

Hamish shook himself and attempted to stand.

"Oh no!" he cried. "What am I going to do now?"

Maybe Badger the Mystical Mutt can use his magic to fix my fur? He wondered.

Hamish crawled hopefully back through the crack in the fence. Badger was fast asleep again.

"Badger, please wake up," whispered Hamish.

Badger shifted himself and raised one eyebrow lazily.

"This had better be good, Hamish. I was enjoying the most scrumptious dream of higgledy piggledy towers of toast," said Badger, and then spotted Hamish's new hairstyle.

"My goodness, you look like a thistle! Did Top Dog do that?"

Hamish nodded.

"Did you tell him what I told you to say?"

"I didn't get a chance. They just came at me with scissors and held me down.

"Okay," sighed Badger. "Let's see what we can do. Follow me."

He marched to the bottom of the garden to a dusty old plant pot and rummaged inside.

"Aha!" exclaimed Badger. "This is exactly what I need."

"What are you doing?" asked Hamish worriedly.

"I am creating an ancient hair-restoring spell, which was passed onto me by Great-Auntie Thistle D'hu. Watch and learn!"

Badger produced a handful of sticks and some slimy goo and placed them on Hamish's head.

"Keep very still," said Badger, "and listen.

"Snail trails and silver-birch sap,
work together and hair will grow back!"

Badger stood back expectantly, Hamish's eyes widened … and nothing happened.

"Need to try it again!" said Badger.

He repeated the spell but this time, more loudly:

"Snail trails and silver-birch sap,
work together
and hair will grow back!"

He stood back and waited.

Hamish waited.

The snail trails slid down Hamish's snout… but his spikes remained.

"It's a really old spell and I haven't done it for a very long time," said Badger apologetically.

Hamish sighed heavily.

"Never mind, Badger. Thanks for trying."

Hamish trotted wearily into the lane, his tummy rumbling and his ears dripping goo.

Suddenly, his nose began to twitch as he sensed that something, or someone, was following him. He turned round sharply, but all he could see was the old bin lid he had used as an earlier disguise, rattling against the fence.

He turned, slid on the slime, tripped over his ears and landed flat on his back. In the kerfuffle of getting to his feet, he bumped awkwardly into Top Dog's legs. He looked up… just in time to see the gang tip a large pot of paint all over him.

Chapter Four

As sticky, thick, blue paint landed on Hamish's head and slid slowly down his long floppy ears, he heard Top Dog, Pogo Paws, Pickle, Dodgy Dave, Snif and Lennie snigger viciously beside him.

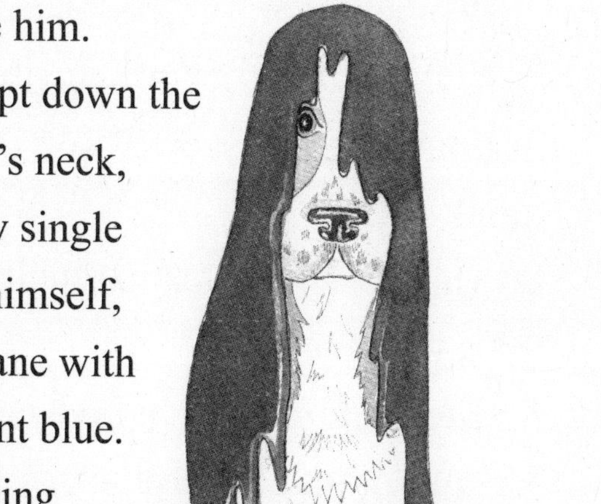

The paint crept down the back of Hamish's neck, sticking to every single hair. He shook himself, splattering the lane with specks of brilliant blue.

"Are you feeling blue?" snarled Dodgy Dave.

"You'll never win *Pet Idol* now, Fancy Pants," sneered Pickle.

"Roses are red, Hamish is blue, who would vote for a loser like you?" bounced Pogo Paws, before adding further insult with: "Pooperscoopersmellysnooper."

Hamish hung his head, dripping big drops of blue paint onto his front paws.

"You're just jealous because you're not in the competition," he said quietly.

"Oh, is that so? You actually think we're jealous of *you*?" scoffed Top Dog. "I don't think so!"

Hamish shook again, sending torpedoes of blue over the gang.

Meanwhile, back in Badger's garden, his dreams of higgledly-piggledy towers of toast were interrupted once more, by the commotion in the lane.

He padded to the bottom of the garden to

peer through the crack in the fence.

All the greenery was *blue,* and he could see Top Dog and his gang circling Hamish.

Right, this calls for drastic action, thought Badger.

He straightened his legs and wagged his bottom until his tail began to whirr. Soon he was hovering above the ground. His big paws climbed the air and he rose higher and higher until he was over the fence and directly above Hamish.

"It's raining cats and dogs, minus the cats," shouted Top Dog, as he looked up and saw what was causing the big shadow over Hamish.

Badger attempted to land, but instead of a graceful swoop, he dropped slap bang on top of Hamish, right in the middle of Top Dog's gang.

"Ooooooooooooouch!" squealed Hamish.

"Quick gang … scarper!" ordered Top Dog.

"Oops!" said Badger, "I did warn you about my landing skills. But at least that's got rid of them."

Hamish pointed a paw at Badger and giggled.

"Well, you certainly came *out of the blue!"*

Badger looked down at his paws and his chest and saw that his thick fur was now also covered in the same blue paint as Hamish.

"I think it's time for my special paint-removing spell," offered Badger.

Just then, they both felt something grab the scruff of their necks. Top Dog and Dodgy Dave had returned.

"Let's get this washed off for you, boys!"

Badger and Hamish were dragged along to the garden at the very end of the lane, to a big, rectangular tank of very smelly, slimy water.

"You're first, Hamish. We need to have you

looking your best for the *Pet Idol* final, don't we?" said Top Dog, and threw him in. Dodgy Dave lifted Badger up and did the same.

"Pooperscoopersmellysnooper!" said Badger and Hamish, screwing up their noses at the horrible stench.

"Goodbye, losers!" laughed Top Dog and Dodgy Dave as they ran off.

Hamish looked miserably at Badger and asked: "Have you any magic to get us out of this one?"

"Er, I'm thinking of a plan," said

Badger.

Hamish's tummy rumbled again.

"I've still not had any dinner," he whined.

"Dinner is least of your worries right now, Hamish. We need to get you cleaned up. I've got a marvellous spell which might just work. It's a mix of wood varnish, soap sage and salt. Hang on to my tail and I'll pull us out of this stinky mess."

Hamish looked at him suspiciously, but hopeful of a glossy coat.

As they trotted up the lane, Hamish's nose began to twitch.

"I can smell cheese," he said. "I love cheese."

His tummy gurgled.

Badger was deep in thought, muttering about the ingredients he needed for his amazing paint-removing spell. He didn't notice that Hamish had fallen behind.

He was following a trail of cheese balls. Crunching each delicious morsel as he went, his nose followed the track all the way to the most beautiful sight he had ever seen — a huge pyramid of cheese balls waiting just for him.

"Yippee!" said Hamish, launching himself at the feast before him.

There was a loud bang and everything went black.

"Caught you, Fancy Pants!" screamed Top Dog. "Where's your pal now?"

"Where am I?" yelped Hamish.

"You're in the best place for pretty boys like you; the wheelie bin. We've dog-napped you, and you're not getting out till after the *Pet Idol* final."

"But what about my dinner?"

But Hamish's yelps were not heard. Top Dog and his gang ran off, the *Mwahahahaha,*

*Mwahahahahahahahahaha*s of their laughter fading into the distance.

Chapter Five

Badger arrived back at his garden. He turned round to tell Hamish the final magic ingredient of the superduper spell he was about to conjure up.

"Where did he go?"

Top Dog and his gang were leaving pee-mails all over the lamp posts in the lane, boasting of their triumph.

Badger re-traced his and Hamish's earlier paw prints. As he stopped to leave a pee-mail of his own, asking for help in locating Hamish, he picked up the pee-mail from Top Dog.

Oh no! Thought Badger. I need to find him before the *Pet Idol* final.

He continued to where the wheelie bins were lined up in a row, and heard an enormous rumble coming from the middle bin.

He edged closer and listened.

There was another rumble and a groan; the unmistakable sound of Hamish's tummy.

"Hamish? Is that you? Are you in there?" asked Badger.

"Badger, help me out. I still haven't had my

dinner and it's really dark in here."

Right, thought Badger. This calls for some help from 'Chief.

He looked down at his red spotty neckerchief and whispered:

"Show koo ray, Show koo ray.

Over to you, 'Chief. Free him today."

The knot of Badger's neckerchief began to unravel slowly and then shot quickly into the air, before billowing out to form a perfect parachute.

Badger closed his eyes and concentrated very hard. Sparkles of light appeared around his nose. His ears pointed forward at the handles on top of the wheelie bin and he stared with all his might.

The lid sprang open, and 'Chief glided inside. Seconds later, the neckerchief emerged with Hamish hanging on below.

"Well done, 'Chief. Gently does it," said

Badger, watching Hamish float softly down to the ground. "It's time for action. This can't go on with Top Dog and his gang. We need to get to the bottom of it, and I think I know who can help. Follow me!"

Back in his garden, Badger sat down on the grass, became very still and sniffed the air. He looked up to where the sun hung in the sky and listened, cocking his head gently from side to side.

Hamish looked on in wonder. Then, out of the corner of his eye, he noticed something he hadn't seen before.

"What's that?" he asked, pointing his paw at what looked like a stone pillar with a stone plate balanced on top.

"That," replied Badger, "is my sundial. Not just any sundial, It's a badgical magical sundial, and, if we're quick, it will take us to meet Baby Unicorn."

"Who? What? Where…?"

"Come here," whispered Badger.

Together, they reached up to look at the plate on top of the pillar. There, in front of them, was the most beautiful arrangement of golden stars, words, numbers and symbols, with a brass pointer in the middle. Hamish craned his neck to read the words.

"Time stays long enough for anyone who will use it. What does that mean?"

Badger smiled.

"We are currently 'here', Hamish, but soon we will be 'there'. And for a moment, time, as we know it, will stand still."

"Wow!" said Hamish, then scratched his head with his paw and asked:

"Does that include dinnertime?"

"Dinnertime too," grinned Badger

"At last!" whispered Hamish.

"Now…" said Badger, "see the sun up

above?"

Hamish nodded, squinting his eyes to look up into the sky.

"The sundial's pointer casts a shadow from the sun, and when that shadow is perfectly aligned between the bone symbol and the ball symbol, then the magic happens and we can take flight."

"But it's nearly there," said Hamish excitedly

"Precisely."

They waited and watched for what seemed like a very long time indeed, until suddenly the shadow glided into place. At exactly that moment, a strange-looking contraption appeared before them, huffing and puffing, clanking and clunking.

Hamish stared.

"What…" he stuttered, "is…" he spluttered, "that?"

Badger looked calmly over his shoulder and said, "That's the Wim-Wim for a wowser to wind the weather up on a wet day!"

"The Wim-Wim... for a wowser... to wind the weather up... on a wet day? But it's not raining," said Hamish.

"It doesn't have to be," sighed Badger.

"But you said it was."

"No, I didn't. That's just its name, Hamish. Now, get in."

"I'm not going *anywhere* in that!"

"Hamish, you have to. The Wim-Wim will take us where we need to go… now!"

"Is it friendly?"

"Of course. The Wim-Wim is here to help us."

Badger stepped confidently onto the first rung of the ladder, beckoning Hamish to follow him. A big golden key, sticking out from the side of the Wim-Wim started to vibrate loudly, making a noise like a siren. Badger twisted it clockwise with his front paws and the piercing sound stopped.

"What was that?" asked Hamish

"The all-important key," replied Badger. "It likes to feel important."

As Badger stepped into the Wim-Wim, a breeze began to swirl, lifting the leaves and petals from the ground. The Wim-Wim creaked and clattered, panted and puttered.

"Come on, Hamish, or we'll miss our slot," yelled Badger.

Hamish steadied his paws and joined Badger in the Wim-Wim.

The strange contraption cranked and rattled, jabbered, murmured and droned.

"It's very noisy," shouted Hamish.

"It will settle down in a moment."

Sparkles of light started to twinkle around Badger.

"We're on our way," said Badger. The Wim-Wim sighed and breathed out a steady rumbling hum.

"Now," said Badger, looking at Hamish, who was still a bit wobbly, "this is the really important part. Are you ready? Close your eyes and repeat after me: *Open our hearts with our eyes closed tight.*"

"Open our hearts with our eyes closed tight," repeated Hamish, closing his eyes tightly.

"Imagine our bodies filling with light."

"Imagine our bodies filling with light," repeated Hamish, taking a deep breath.

"With good intentions clearly in sight."

"With good intentions clearly in sight," repeated Hamish, starting to tingle all over.

"Let Badgical Magical Dreams take flight," said Badger, with a flourish. The top of the Wim-Wim started to whirr rapidly.

"Let Badgical Magical Dreams take flight," repeated Hamish, with similar flourish. Just then a wondrous beat pulsed throughout his body.

Chapter Six

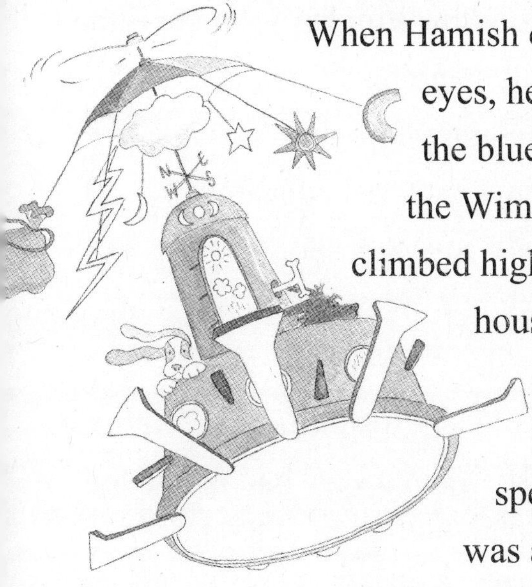

When Hamish opened his eyes, he was high in the blue sky, aboard the Wim-Wim. As they climbed higher and higher, houses became dots, and dots became specks until it was all a bit of a blur.

"Still hanging on, Hamish?" shouted Badger, over the whizz and whistle of the wind.

"Just about, where are we?"

"Nearly There."

"But where *is* Nearly There?"

"You'll find out soon enough. We're going to visit my grumpy friend, Nippy Nimbus. He's the gatekeeper to Nearly There. I've got to make sure the Wim-Wim lands on the right spot. He's usually hanging around at about twenty past the southern Fogbow."

"The southern what?" asked Hamish.

Suddenly, the Wim-Wim shot upwards as Badger caught sight of Nippy Nimbus; a big, fluffy, white cloud.

"Don't be fooled by his fluffiness," warned Badger, "he's usually in a very bad mood and finds everything, including us, ridiculous."

As the Wim-Wim landed clumsily in the misty swirl, an irritated voice shouted out:

"Hey! Get off of my cloud!"

"Oh no," said Badger, scratching his head with his paw. "I've forgotten the password."

"What do you mean?" asked Hamish. "Where are we anyway?"

"Welcome to Nippy Nimbus, the grumpiest cloud in the world," sighed Badger.

Nippy Nimbus bellowed. "I might have known it was you, Badger, the 'full of nonsense' mystical mutt. Can't remember your password, eh? Oh dear, no entry for you today. Go away. Goodbye."

Badger climbed down the Wim-Wim's

ladder and frowned. His eyebrows twitched.

"Ah," he smiled. "Got it, actually," he replied smugly to his bad-tempered friend, Nippy Nimbus. "Try Cloud Number Nine."

Badger shimmied his bottom and crossed his paws in a little dance, as he bounced around the fluffiness feeling very pleased with himself.

"Wrong, Numptie!" cackled Nippy Nimbus

"Oh!" exclaimed Badger, not quite sure what to do next. Hamish clambered out of the Wim-Wim to join Badger.

"Okay… I lied," admitted Nippy Nimbus huffily.

A parting suddenly appeared within the depths of the white mist.

"Come ahead then," said Nippy, "but don't expect it to be the same password next time. I'll catch you out yet!"

The important key on the side of the Wim-

Wim started to glow brightly again.

"C'mon Hamish, let's crank up the Wim-Wim. Nippy's letting us through."

Badger climbed back into the Wim-Wim, followed hastily by Hamish, then grasped the golden key with his paws and pushed it until it started to whirr on its own.

The Wim-Wim creaked and clattered and panted and puttered before shooting through the gap in the mist at alarming speed.

When the Wim-Wim landed, Hamish was thrown on top of Badger, who was feeling a bit dazed after the speedy descent.

Hamish rubbed his eyes in bewilderment. They were in a luscious green forest. Birds sang, water trickled and the air smelled zingily fresh. The branches of the trees bent and bowed to welcome them, and plants shot up to say "hello".

"Amazing!" shrieked Hamish.

They set off on the golden-leaved path in front of them. As Hamish looked at the wise old trees and the shimmer of sunlight upon their leaves, he asked:

"Is this an *enchanted* forest, Badger?"

Before Badger could answer, they heard a rustle nearby.

"Ssssshhhh," whispered Badger gently. "I think Baby Unicorn is coming out to play."

"Baby who?"

Out of the trees, a pure white creature appeared with a glowing spiral horn on its forehead. Its eyes were deep pools of kindness and its mane was long, flowing and silky.

"That's a funny looking horse. Why has it got a horn in the middle of its head?" asked Hamish.

"That's not just any horse, Hamish. It's a unicorn and that horn is magical. It can purify the darkest poison, protect from harm, heal a broken heart and help people to see things clearly."

"Wow, do you think it can clean us up too?" whispered Hamish, who was still a bit whiffy from earlier.

The unicorn's horn started to sparkle.

"Let's see," replied Badger.

Baby Unicorn walked towards them, stopped at their feet and bowed its horn at them both.

Hamish followed Badger's lead and bowed back.

"Yuck!" said Baby Unicorn. "You smell!"

"Sorry about that," said Badger, blushing.

"We had an unfortunate encounter with some grime and slime."

"Okay, stand back both of you."

From Baby Unicorn's horn, a blast of hot, soapy bubbles shot forth and covered Hamish and Badger from head to toe. They shook themselves and looked at each other. Every trace of blue paint, snail trails and slime, goo and gunge had gone.

"Well, that's certainly better than my paint-removing spell!" said Badger in admiration.

"All part of the job," said Baby Unicorn.

"What happens now?" whispered the now squeaky-clean and perfectly groomed Hamish.

"We follow," winked Badger.

The unicorn turned and headed off down the golden-leaved path. They followed for what seemed like a long time, until a shaft of light appeared through a clearing. Baby Unicorn turned towards the light with Badger and Hamish close behind.

Everything was hushed but for the twigs and the bracken snapping and crackling beneath their feet.

They passed a signpost pointing ahead. On it, in big lettering, it said: "Nearly There".

Badger looked back at Hamish and said:

"Remember when you asked me earlier where 'Nearly There' was? There's the signpost, so we're very close…"

"But we've been walking for aaaaaages," moaned Hamish.

"To quote a well-known saying, Hamish," said Badger, wisely, "'You never can tell how close you are. It may be near though it seems so far.' Come on, we truly are 'Nearly There', which means the next bit is 'There.'"

"Okay, but 'There' seems an awfully long way away from 'Here'."

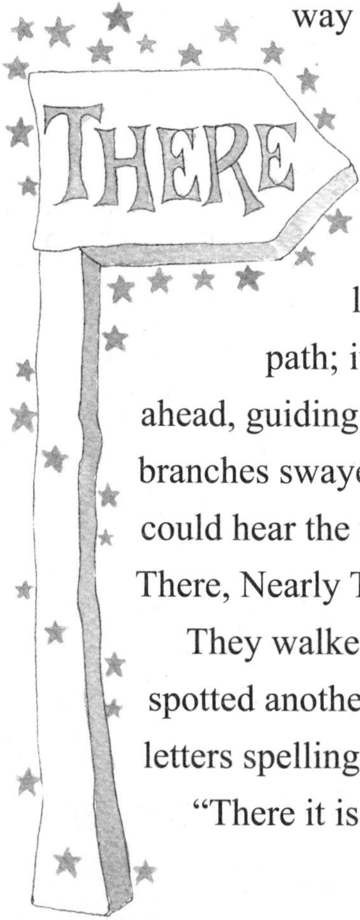

"Patience now, Hamish, we're so close."

A big old tree leaned over Hamish's path; its branches pointed ahead, guiding him onwards. As the branches swayed, Hamish was sure he could hear the tree whisper, "Nearly There, Nearly There."

They walked on until Badger spotted another sign with even larger letters spelling out the word 'There'.

"There it is. We've found 'There'."

"There, at last," sighed Hamish, hearing his tummy rumble and hoping that Badger was right about dinnertime standing still.

They passed through an archway of trees and spied the mouth of a cave set in a cliff of clear quartz crystal. The entrance dazzled, twinkled and glimmered with a brilliant light.

A sign outside read:

Thank you for coming here to There, which is now, of course, "Here".

We hope you enjoy your visit.

Come back soon, and don't forget to tell all of your friends "Here, There and Everywhere."

"So, here we are at There, which is also 'here' without the T," said Badger, looking at Hamish knowingly.

"No tea? Is that the same as dinner?" asked Hamish, with a worried look.

"Don't worry, Hamish, it's not that kind of

tea. Dinnertime will still be There when we get back."

"Brilliant!" replied Hamish, in wide-eyed

wonder, wondering what could possibly be inside the cave.

They walked towards the opening. Baby Unicorn motioned for them to follow.

“Amazing!” shouted Hamish as he weaved his way through different coloured crystal stalagmites and stalactites. His voice and the word “amazing” bounced back at him as they echoed round the walls of the cave.

“Wow!” shrieked Hamish

“Wow, wow, wow, wow, wow, wow…” replied the echo.

“There’re lots of Hamishes in here,” said Hamish, a bit befuddled.

“Ssshhhhhhhhhhhhh,” whispered Badger.

Hamish looked sheepish. As they walked on, he glanced over his shoulder, but could not resist throwing a final word to the cave.

“Dinner!”

“Dinner, dinner, dinner, dinner, dinner,

dinner…"

Hamish smiled to himself and followed Badger and Baby Unicorn, who had been waiting patiently for him to finish his fun.

Chapter Seven

Baby Unicorn stopped and nodded to Badger, who stepped forward and nodded respectfully back.

"My friend Hamish here is in a spot of bother. Can you help us, please?" asked Badger hopefully.

Baby Unicorn bowed his head.

Hamish watched in wonder.

The unicorn pointed his horn towards the back of the cave, where the rock was unusually flat and smooth.

"Right," said Badger to Hamish. "Are you sitting comfortably? Watch this."

A blast of light exploded from Baby

Unicorn's horn, and little by little, the light took shape on the cave wall.

There, lit up in front of them was an image of a puppy behind metal bars in a pen. Many Big Folk passed backwards and forwards but didn't stop to look in. Then two of them stopped and pointed. The puppy ran up to

the bars and barked excitedly. The Big Folk chatted with each other and disappeared.

"Oh, they look a bit like my Big Folk," said Hamish excitedly.

"Sssh," said Badger. "concentrate Hamish."

Hamish fixed his gaze on the cave wall.

Outside the pen, the Big Folk returned with the Dog Catcher. The puppy's ears pinned back, his tail stopped wagging and he stepped away from the bars. Two huge gloved hands curled around the metal bars, and the puppy cowered in the corner. The Dog Catcher unlocked the cage and lifted the puppy into the arms of the waiting Big Folk.

"He's been saved," said Hamish.

There was a crackle on the screen, and now the puppy was alone in a lane— not unlike the lane at the bottom of Hamish's garden — and his Big Folk were nowhere to be seen. The dog was now being chased by the Dog

Catcher.

There was another crackle on the screen and there was a picture of Top Dog.

"Oh," said Hamish, surprised. "It's Top Dog! Does Baby Unicorn know him?"

"Baby Unicorn knows everyone and everything."

"Right. Okay." Hamish's tail started to wag.

On the wall they saw Top Dog shivering in a cardboard box, whining for some food and still on the run from the Dog Catcher.

"Oh, he looks so sad and lonely. Why is he living in a box? Why has he got no food? Where are his Big Folk?" asked Hamish.

"I don't think he's got any Big Folk any more, Hamish."

"But who gives him his dinner?" asked Hamish

"No one," replied Badger, then added,

"Maybe that's another reason why Top Dog wants to stop you from entering *Pet Idol*? He sees you going home for dinner every night, going for walks with your Big Folk, and having a warm bed and toys. Perhaps he's chasing you because he's afraid of being chased by the Dog Catcher."

"He looks so thin," said Hamish quietly.

There was another crackle on the screen. There in front of him, was Hamish on a stage with lots of Big Folk cheering.

"Who's that?" he asked. "His ears are as long as mine."

"That's because it *is* you. Hamish," said Badger gently.

"But I don't understand. If I'm here, how can I be there, and if I'm supposed to be there, how am I here? And this is 'There' so how can I possibly be here at all?"

Hamish furrowed his brow.

"Sometimes," said Badger, even more gently, "we are lucky enough to get a glimpse of how things might be, not just today, but tomorrow and the next day, and the next day, and then the next day too."

"Oh," said Hamish in a very small voice.

"It looks like you're going to win that show, Hamish. Let's see what else we can see."

They peered back into the cave and saw Hamish being presented with his prize at the famous *Pet Idol* Show.

"A year's supply of Crunchy Munchy Chewy Chops and a personalized dinner bowl for you," beamed the Big Folk presenter.

"But why have I won? I didn't even enter it. Between my Big Folk talking about it and Top Dog chasing me because of it, I'm fed up with the whole thing."

"It's more of a Big Folk competition, Hamish. The Big Folk like to compete, and if they can't do it themselves, then they use us… well *you*. Maybe those ears which trip you up all the time, are not just any ears…"

"Are *my* ears badgical magical too?" asked Hamish, wide-eyed.

"Watch," said Badger, smiling.

The picture went blank. Baby Unicorn turned around to face them, his horn still aglow.

"What happens next?" asked Hamish,

aware of another large rumble coming from his tummy. "I feel really hungry after seeing those Crunchy Munchy Chewy Chops. It must be dinnertime!"

"Don't worry, Hamish. When we get back, dinnertime will still be some time off."

Hamish looked puzzled.

"But my tummy thinks it should be now."

Just then, another rumbling hum startled them from outside the cave.

"Patience, Hamish. Sounds like the Wim-Wim has arrived to take us home, so it won't be long," said Badger comfortingly "But first, there's one more thing Baby Unicorn might be able to help us with."

Sparkles of light appeared around Badger's nose as he looked knowingly at the unicorn's horn.

"Close your eyes, Hamish," said Baby Unicorn, as he directed his glowing horn towards the little spaniel's spiky tufts.

Hamish felt a ticklish sensation on top of his head. When he opened his eyes, he knew at once, that his slapdash haircut had been restored to its former glory.

"Thank you so much," said Hamish.

Baby Unicorn turned and led them out of the cave where the Wim-Wim was cranking and panting.

Badger bowed politely to Baby Unicorn, grabbed Hamish's paw and they stepped inside the Wim-Wim.

"Right Hamish, here we go. Close your eyes and repeat after me: Open our hearts with our eyes closed tight…"

Seconds later, Badger said softly, "It's okay, Hamish. We're back in plenty of time for dinner. You can open your eyes now."

Hamish opened his eyes and there they were, back at the sundial, near the crack in the fence, at the bottom of Badger's garden.

"Awesome!" said Hamish. "What just happened?"

"We've been on a badgical magical adventure." said Badger. "And now I need some toast."

Before Badger turned to trot indoors, he saw Hamish perch up on his hind legs to look once more at the sundial. He looked round bewildered.

"But the shadow hasn't moved!"

Badger looked at Hamish and winked.

Hamish tilted his head and murmured to himself, "Wow. I've been badgical magicalled."

He squeezed through the crack in the fence, sniffed the air with fresh confidence, then ventured into the lane and headed homewards for his dinner.

But it wasn't long before Top Dog and his

gang caught sight of Hamish and fell into step behind him.

Chapter Eight

Hamish looked round. His heart sank.

Top Dog and his gang stood in a line across the lane.

"So, you managed to escape then?" snarled the gang leader. "And your hair's grown back as well. How odd."

"Badger the Mystical Mutt helped me," replied Hamish.

"What are you doing hanging around with that Badger mutt anyway?" barked Top Dog.

"Oooooohhhhhhh. Has Hamish got a new friend now? You're in good company there. Badger's strange too. What is it they call him? Badger the Mystical Mutt? More like

Badger the Neighbourhood Nut," growled Snif menacingly.

"He's not a nut and he's not strange," snapped Hamish, shaking himself angrily. "In fact, he's helped me, to understand why you, Top Dog", Hamish stood facing him, "are so horrible to me."

"Oh, has he really? So it's not because you're an annoying little softie, or because you don't know how to fight without those gangly ears getting in the way, or because you are a goody four paws?"

"He showed me everything. I saw it!"

"Saw what?" snorted Top Dog.

"You! As a pup … in the Dog Catcher's van… in the cage … with the Big Folk … on your own"

"Stop!" scowled Top Dog, looking nervously around. "You'll be going for another dunk in the tank if you don't stop your nonsense. That Badger is even nuttier than I thought. This is ridiculous. I'll sort him out right now."

Top Dog circled the rest of the gang and barked fiercely: "Leave this to me; I'll handle that interfering nut myself."

The gang scarpered, leaving Hamish alone, worrying about what Top Dog would do to his new friend and concerned that he was still not home for his dinner.

Back in the garden, Badger the Mystical Mutt was dreaming, as usual, of higgledly-piggledy towers of toast.

At the crack in the fence, an angry eye peered through.

Top Dog spied Badger out for the count and crept through. Badger budged his bottom to get more comfortable. Top Dog stopped in his tracks. He waited, his sights fixed on his prey.

He edged closer.

Badger's nose started to twitch as a fly hovered close to his nostrils. He shook his head. Top Dog froze and waited, but Badger quickly returned to his slumber.

Now at his side, Top Dog was ready to pounce. He noticed the famous red-spotted neckerchief around his neck and thought: This should be easy …

With that, he leapt at Badger and grabbed him by the scruff of his neck. Badger's eyes flashed open as all thoughts of toast disappeared and he realized that he was under attack.

"You're not so smart now, Badger! Stupid name anyway! You don't even look like a badger!"

Badger tried to free himself from Top Dog's grasp.

"What are you doing trying to fill Hamish's head with nonsense?"

Badger looked down at his red spotty neckerchief and whispered:

"Show koo ray, Show koo ray, over to you, 'Chief, to take him away."

Top Dog loosened his grip as he felt the knot of Badger's neckerchief slowly unravel. He stepped back, confused, as he watched it come completely undone.

The neckerchief shot into the air, spun around, turned sharply, hovered for a moment, then dived straight towards Top Dog, knocking him flat on his back. Within seconds, all of Top Dog's paws, and even his tail, were tied together with the red spotty neckerchief.

Badger rubbed his neck and sat back. "Thanks, 'Chief!"

"What just happened?" whimpered Top Dog, a trifle dazed.

"Sorry about that. Now, are you likely to try that again, or does the 'Chief need to keep you tied up a bit longer?"

"Erm … no. Sorry, I promise … really! Just untie me. Please?"

Badger thought for a moment, and then said:

"Show koo ray, Show koo ray, come back 'Chief, that's enough for today."

The red spotty neckerchief carefully unknotted itself and glided back to fasten again around Badger's neck. Badger tapped it with his paw.

"That's better. Now, what's all this about then? And why should I talk to you after that bath you gave me in the tank?"

Top Dog sat up, keeping a wary distance from Badger.

"Erm … yes, sorry about that. It was Hamish we were after, not you. Hamish says he saw me as a pup. I don't understand. That was years ago, long before he was even born."

"Ah," said Badger gently. "Sometimes, when we look for all the right reasons, we can see things as they really are."

"I'm even more confused now," frowned Top Dog.

"Let me explain then. You're not a bad dog, but from what I understand, you've rarely known, or been shown, any love or kindness. So it must be difficult for you to show love or kindness to anyone else."

Top Dog shook himself gruffly.

"What do you mean?"

"Tell me about your Big Folk? Who feeds you and walks you?"

"I don't have any Big Folk. I don't need any," replied Top Dog defensively.

"Did you ever?"

"Yes, once."

"And did they feed and walk you?"

"They did for a while," admitted Top Dog.

"What happened to them?"

"They moved away."

"Surely you could have moved with them?"

"I ran away while they were packing their cases," said Top Dog sadly. "I went back every night for weeks, but the house was empty."

"So where did you go?" asked Badger

softly.

"Nowhere. I ran around all day and roamed the bins at night. Eventually, the Dog Catcher caught me and put me in a cage. That's where I met Dodgy Dave. He helped me to escape. I've lived on this lane ever since."

"So why are you so horrible to Hamish?" asked Badger

"He just seems to have everything: Big Folk, dinner, walks and somewhere warm to sleep. And as if that wasn't enough, now he's in this *Pet Idol* competition. Because of all the interest in Hamish and the lane, the Dog Catcher is back on my tail."

"That's still no reason to be horrible to him. *Pet Idol* wasn't his fault. Has he ever been horrible to you?"

"No," said Top Dog, hanging his head.

"Does being horrible to Hamish make you feel better?"

"No … not better, but the rest of the gang think I'm great because of it."

"Why don't you try being nice to Hamish and see how that makes you feel? It's a good feeling, and I'll bet that Hamish will be happy to share out his Crunchy Munchy Chewy Chops with his friends if he wins."

"But I can't, because then the gang will think I'm going soft. They'll find a new leader."

"You may lose them, but you will gain a true friend in Hamish. Think about it!" said Badger wisely.

Top Dog grunted and backed towards the crack in the fence with his tail pointing downwards and his ears flat against his head.

Chapter Nine

Badger heard a strange scraping sound coming from the lane. He looked out to see Hamish dragging his dinner bowl full of Buddy Bites towards Top Dog's cardboard box.

That pup learned a lot about kindness in the crystal cave, Badger smiled to himself.

Top Dog looked up angrily then spotted a clothes peg holding Hamish's ears together. He sniggered to himself.

"What are you up to, Peg Ears? Are you back for another thumping?" growled Top Dog.

"I wondered if you wanted some of this," said Hamish.

Top Dog's mouth watered as his eyes feasted upon the overflowing bowl of juicy chunky Buddy Bites, but before he could tuck in, his pride took over.

"What? Eat with the likes of you? Mummy's Boy, who has to have his ears pegged back while he's eating? Don't think so. Beat it!" said Top Dog gruffly.

"It's a shame if it goes to waste," ventured Hamish hesitantly. "As for the peg, that was my Big Folk's idea. The *Pet Idol final* is tomorrow and my ears keep dangling in my dinner, which I like, because it's good for afters, but they say it makes a mess."

"But you're a dog! Mess is good," said Top Dog. Then he shook himself and got back to being gruff and tough. "Well, I've got to admire your spirit, Fancy Pants. You've had a few beatings already, and here you are looking for another."

"Look, why don't I just leave it here. If you don't want it, then maybe the birds will eat it."

With that, Hamish bounded his way back to the fence to join Badger out of Top Dog's view. Top Dog sniffed at the food, looked around him then, grudgingly took a few bites … then a few more … then a few more … until he had hungrily wolfed down the lot.

Hamish smiled at Badger.

"Hamish, where are you?" shouted a voice from a nearby garden.

"Oh, that's my Big Folk, I'd better go," said Hamish, and trotted home.

Top Dog tilted his head to one side, with a flicker of recognition when he heard Hamish's Big Folk call him inside.

Even after all these years, he thought

fondly, I still think I can hear their voices.

He shook himself; he was probably just being silly. He returned to licking the empty dinner bowl then licked around it again. Only when he was totally sure the bowl had no more licks left, did he sit back and think.

"Could it be possible that my own Big Folk have been right here in the lane, under my nose, all this time?" he wondered.

He shook himself again.

"That's ridiculous," he thought "One chinwag with that mystical mutt and I'm getting soppy. I'll take this back to that daft peg-eared spaniel."

He dragged the bowl back into the lane and up to the garden where Hamish lived. When he arrived, Hamish asked him timidly:

"Why are you so annoyed about me being in *Pet Idol?"*

"I hate everything it stands for. All those

posh pampered pets and their posh pampered Big Folk. It's nonsense!"

"But I'm not posh, or pampered, I'm just Hamish with daft ears."

"You said it!"

"So what's it all about then?" asked Hamish innocently.

"Stupid pets, stupid judges, stupid prize. Winner takes it all."

"Prize? What's the prize? Can I eat it?" asked Hamish excitedly.

"Who says you're going to win?" sneered Top Dog. "According to the pee-mail I just read, you're up against Polly Poodle and Treacle the tortoise-shell cat."

"Then again …" added Top Dog thoughtfully, "against those two, you've got a pretty good chance."

"I like Polly Poodle and Treacle's one of my best friends."

"That doesn't surprise me," said Top Dog, raising his eyes to the sky. "Anyway, since you asked, the prize is a year's supply of Crunchy Munchy Chewy Chops and your very own personalized dinner bowl. Big Deal!"

"Brilliant!" said Hamish, "although there's only so many Crunchy Munchy Chewy Chops even I could eat in a year. I'd have to share them out."

"Why would you want to do that?" asked Top Dog.

"Why not?" replied Hamish.

Top Dog shrugged, turned to leave, then said over his shoulder:

"Thanks for the dinner, by the way. You're not as bad as I thought."

"Neither are you," said Hamish.

"Sssssssssshhhhhhhhh! I've got my reputation to think of."

As Top Dog headed homewards to his

cardboard box, Hamish ran indoors with his dinner bowl, happier than he'd been in a while.

He didn't trip over his ears once.

The next day, the neighbourhood pets and strays clustered eagerly around the window of the local TV shop. It was the end of the live final of *Pet Idol* and all eyes were on the TV screens inside.

Soon the moment came that they had all been waiting for … the loud speaker outside the shop announced in a Big Folk voice …

"In third place, it's Polly the Poodle for her perfect poodle perm and particularly posh poise."

The audience gasped.

"No surprise there, gang," scoffed Snif. "Her Big Folk spend a fortune at the Poodle

Parlour."

Dodgy Dave added: "She looks like candy floss on legs."

Top Dog, who was watching from the side away from his gang, looked over and shook his head.

"Is there any need for that, you lot?" he asked.

"But it's exactly what you would usually say. What's changed?" asked Dodgy Dave, a little bamboozled, before adding,

"Why aren't you standing here with us anyway?"

"Yes, when exactly did you start being so nicey-wicey?" barked Lennie.

"Especially about those losers!" added Pickle, nodding at the TV.

Top Dog ignored them all and returned to the screen. The gang did the same.

"And in second place, we have Treacle the tortoise-shell cat, for her tender treatment of other cats."

The crowd outside gasped again.

"Ah, Treacle. I'm so glad. She deserves it. She's such a gentle soul," sighed Badger the Mystical Mutt, who was watching quietly from the back of the crowd.

Top Dog and Badger shared a quick smile with each other.

"What?" Pickle screamed at the screen, "Treacle the tortoise-shell cat? Are you mad? She's a worn-out goody-two-shoes moggie!"

Top Dog growled at Pickle menacingly:

"Leave it!"

Pickle looked at the rest of the gang in disbelief.

"Did you just hear that? Am I having a nightmare, or did *that* really happen? Is it just me, or is *he,"* Pickle nodded in Top Dog's direction, "acting very strangely?"

Pogo Paws, Dodgy Dave, Snif and Lennie all grunted in agreement, each as baffled as the other as to why Top Dog wasn't joining in with their jokes.

Then, the voice from the loud speaker boomed out again, and all the animals outside hushed.

"And now, for the big one..."

There was a very long pause.

"The one you've all been waiting for..."

Another long pause.

"...the one who will tonight take away this year's *Pet Idol* trophy..."

There was another long pause.

"How long is this going to take? Get on with it!" yelled Dodgy Dave.

"…the one who will also receive a fabulous prize of a year's supply of Crunchy Munchy Chewy Chops…"

"Is this likely to finish tonight? I've got a bone to pick," sighed Snif.

"…as well as a personalized dinner bowl…"

"Oh, pooperscoopersmellysnooper! Just tell us the blooming winner. I'm bored now," grumbled Pogo Paws.

"At last, in first place, the winner of this year's *Pet Idol,* is…"

The drum roll seemed to go on forever. Top Dog stared at the screen. Badger hoped with all his heart that Hamish would be the winner.

Top Dog's gang — Pogo Paws, Pickle, Dodgy Dave, Snif and Lennie — all sat, scowling at the screen. It seemed like an age before the Big Folk's voice finally announced:

"HAMISH! We've chosen Hamish for his

happy heart, not to mention his helpful and honest nature, and his ability to listen to others with his huge floppy ears."

Hamish bounced up to the stage to collect his award from the Big Folk. His tail was wagging so much that his bottom shook.

Outside the TV shop, the collected animals were barking and woofing, meowing and purring, squeaking and chirping in merriment. Pogo Paws, Pickle, Dodgy Dave, Snif and Lennie were booing and growling. Top Dog stared at them all coldly.

"Why can't you be pleased for Hamish? He's going to share his prize with us all."

"Oh, sorry, Top Dog. Is this the same Hamish you were chasing a few days ago, tying his ears on top of his head and cutting his hair?" snarled Dodgy Dave.

"Yes, the same Hamish you were joyfully covering in blue paint and dunking in the tank?" barked a peeved Pickle.

"And the same Hamish you were calling a floppy-eared softie and Fancy Pants recently?" added Snif.

"Yes, I know," admitted Top Dog, "but things have changed. I was wrong. He's not a bad pup, and once you get to know him, he's okay really."

Dodgy Dave looked at the rest of the gang and they nodded knowingly.

"Top Dog, I think it's time for us to split. We can't be in your gang anymore. You're turning into a *pet*. Why don't you be friends with that floppy-eared softie and I'll set up a new gang … with me in charge!"

Top Dog shrugged, then he noticed one of the Big Folk up a ladder, cleaning windows with a great big bucket of soapy water. The one-time leader of the gang walked over and nudged the bottom rung. The bucket toppled and spilled soapy suds all over Dodgy Dave.

Dodgy Dave was rooted to the spot as he dripped frothy bubbles all over the pavement. Then, realizing what had just happened, he shook himself vigorously, pointed his paw in rage and growled menacingly:

"Just you wait, Top Dog. We'll make sure the Dog Catcher gets you this time. Come on, gang!"

With that, the gang ran off.

Chapter Eleven

Top Dog returned to his cardboard box with his head hung low and his tail down. He was happy for Hamish's win, yet sad that his pals had deserted him.

"Well, Badger said this might happen," he sighed. "They weren't ever really my pals. They were only interested in making everyone else unhappy and I don't want to do that anymore. Leading the gang was beginning to feel like a chore anyway. They can look after themselves from now on."

For the first time since he had left his Big Folk, he nosed something out from the back of his cardboard box; something which he had been given as a pup. Something he had managed to keep with him through thick and thin; a scrawny, grey, matted cuddly toy. He pulled his scruffy blanket around him and bedded down for a nap. He fell into a contented dream about his old family of Big Folk and a new friend called Hamish.

Tucked in tight and nuzzled close to him was his trusty unicorn toy.

Meanwhile, as Hamish headed homewards with his prize, he decided to visit Top Dog to share out his Crunchy Munchy Chewy Chops. He resolved to keep his personalized dinner bowl for himself because, after all, who could he possibly share it with when it had his name on it?

As he trotted cheerfully up the lane, five ominous shadows surrounded him and merged into a menacing circle. Hamish looked from left to right from front to back and, holding on tightly to his prize, started to panic.

"Aren't you going to share out your Crunchy Munchy Chewy Chops with us then, Fancy Pants?" snarled Dodgy Dave, emerging from the shadows.

The hairs on the back of Hamish's neck sprang upright and beads of sweat bubbled on the end of his nose. He quivered.

"Enjoying the spotlight, eh?" spat Snif.

"Just hand over the Chewy Chops," hissed Pickle right into Hamish's ear. Hamish winced.

"Lost your tongue, Pretty Boy?" snarled

Lennie.

"Just give us the Chewy Chops and you can be on your way," hissed Pickle again.

"No! Go away!" squealed Hamish, as Pogo Paws bounced forward about to swipe his precious bag of Crunchy Munchy Chewy

Chops.

Out of nowhere, another shadow launched into the middle of the circle, knocking Pogo Paws to the ground.

"Run, Hamish!" shouted Top Dog, as the gang closed in on their old leader.

Hamish ran as fast as he could, still clinging tightly to his prize. As he ran, he heard the yelps and thuds, the screams and whimpers, the howls and barks of a pack of savage dogs and their prey.

I need to get Badger, he panicked, as he ran towards the crack in the fence at the bottom of his garden.

"Badger!" shouted Hamish. "Badger, where are you?"

But Badger wasn't there.

Suddenly, a voice boomed from above. "Hello, Hamish. Well done! I knew you could do it. Even Top Dog was cheering you on."

Hamish looked around him.

"Up here," shouted Badger

Hamish looked up to see Badger in the treetop, covered in leaves.

He grinned sheepishly at Hamish.

"I was trying out a new teleporting spell, but it needs more practice."

"Badger, hurry up, there's no time to waste. Top Dog's life is in serious danger. You need to come down now and help me save him before it's too late," panted a very flustered Hamish.

"What? What's happened?"

"Follow me, and bring all the magic you

can. We're going to need it."

As they reached the spot where Hamish had been ambushed, they found Top Dog lying motionless.

"Oh no!" cried Hamish "We're too late."

Top Dog whimpered. Hamish ran to him and nuzzled him.

Badger looked up the lane and spotted the Dog Catcher's van.

"Quick Hamish, we've got to get Top Dog away from here," he said anxiously.

Top Dog groaned.

"I don't think he can move," said Hamish, worriedly.

"Right, we need to think quickly."

The Dog Catcher's heavy boots thundered down the lane.

Badger spied a pile of grass cuttings, and nodded to Hamish. The two of them stood in the middle of the heap, and kicked their

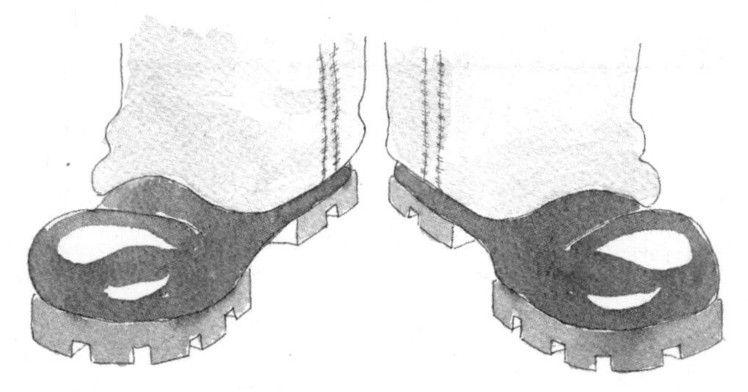

back legs as fast as they could, showering the grass over Top Dog until he was completely covered.

"Look as cute and calm as you can, Hamish, and I'll try to distract him."

The Dog Catcher stopped when he saw Hamish and bent down to ruffle his fur.

"Congratulations on winning *Pet Idol.* I wish all dogs were like you," he said gruffly.

Hamish gave him a huge smile and fluttered his long eye lashes.

"Right, I'm after that rogue, Top Dog, so I must get on."

Suddenly, the pile of grass cuttings behind

Hamish sneezed. The Dog Catcher stopped and looked around.

Quick as a flash, Badger barked loudly and ran towards the other end of the lane. The Dog Catcher followed him.

Phew! thought Hamish, That was close.

Minutes later, a panting Badger returned.

"I led him in the direction of Dodgy Dave's hidey hole. That should give us enough time to get Top Dog back to his box. But first we need to take a look at his injuries."

Badger and Hamish gently pulled him free of the grass cuttings.

"Oh dear, it's worse than I thought," sighed Badger, looking at Top Dog's broken shape. "We must act quickly before we can move him anywhere.

"First, Hamish, I need you to be absolutely still and silent, while I ask 'Chief to help us heal his wounds."

Badger placed a paw softly on Top Dog's shoulder. Sparkles of light appeared and swirled around their friend. 'Chief unravelled slowly from around Badger's neck and floated onto Top Dog, as he whispered:

"Show Koo Ray, Show Koo Ray, Show Koo Ray.

Use your healing magic to take the pain away."

Top Dog lifted his head. His eye was swollen, his ear was bitten and crusted and one of his front paws was badly twisted.

Badger's 'Chief tied itself around Top Dog's paw, as the sparkles of light faded.

"Do you think you could walk a little bit now?" asked Badger gently. "We just need to get you back to your bed, before the Dog Catcher returns."

Top Dog nodded heavily and tried to get up.

"Okay, Hamish. One shoulder each. Let's go!"

Together, they carried their poor injured pal back to his cardboard box.

"He should be okay for a while there," said Badger, as they walked wearily home, "but the Dog Catcher *will* be back for him."

Chapter Twelve

All the earlier excitement of *Pet Idol* had been forgotten.

Badger and Hamish sat in the garden, wondering how poor Top Dog could ever escape the Dog Catcher.

"He's normally so big and strong, but now he has no fight left in him," said Hamish.

"If only he had a home where he could rest properly and get better," said Badger.

"He doesn't even get his dinner every night," added Hamish.

"If he had a home, he'd get his dinners every night," Badger replied.

"It won't be long until the Dog Catcher finds

him in that cardboard box," frowned Hamish.

"But not if he had a home," said Badger.

"You saw in the Crystal Cave what it was like for him growing up," said Hamish.

"I know, but it would be different if he had a home," Badger replied.

"Top Dog hasn't even got any Big Folk to look after him," Hamish added.

"But he would if he had a home," winked Badger.

Badger's eyebrows began to twitch magically. Hamish looked at Badger.

"Do you think he needs a home?" asked Hamish.

"It would certainly help him right now," smiled Badger.

"Maybe I've just had an idea," said Hamish. "I've got to go."

As Hamish squeezed through the crack in the fence at the bottom of the garden, Badger coughed loudly.

"Ahem… before you go. Did you mention something about sharing out your Crunchy Munchy Chewy Chops?"

Back at home, Hamish sniffed around for his lead and favourite squeaky ball.

This should do the trick, he thought as he squeaked his toy with gusto at his Big Folk's feet.

"Okay, Hamish!" his Big Folk shouted. "We get the message. It's a bit late but come on then. It's not every day you win first prize in *Pet Idol*. Let's go for a walk."

Soon Hamish was trotting down the lane towards where Top Dog lived in his cardboard box.

Now's my chance to help *him*, he thought.

Hamish excitedly drew his Big Folk closer and closer towards the cardboard box.

But when they got there, it was empty.

Top Dog was nowhere to be seen.

Oh no, thought Hamish, the Dog Catcher must have captured him.

He lay down beside the empty box and whimpered.

"C'mon Hamish," said his Big Folk tugging at his lead. "It's only an old empty box. Let's go home so you can enjoy your treats."

Hamish moped homewards and resolved to return in the morning. For once, he had no appetite — his tummy was in knots.

The next day, Hamish dragged his Big Folk back to the same spot, but still there was no sign of Top Dog.

I wonder if Badger the Mystical Mutt can help me find him? Hamish thought hopefully.

He peered through the crack in the fence and saw Badger drooling over a slice of toast.

"Badger," he shouted "Top Dog's gone!"

"Gone?" said Badger

"He's not in his cardboard box. The Dog Catcher must have caught him"

"Well, let's see," said Badger looking back to the slice of toast.

He peered into the crispy, butter-drenched slice. Slowly something started to appear out of the burnt bit in the middle of the bread. It was a big black bin shape.

"He's hiding in the wheelie bin," revealed Badger smugly.

"Thanks Badger, you really are mystical," said Hamish, turning on his heels to fetch his Big Folk.

Hamish and his Big Folk approached the upturned sideways wheelie bin. Top Dog was breathing heavily. His eye was still swollen, one ear was still crusted, and his twisted paw still had Badger's 'Chief tied around it.

Hamish nuzzled up to him and noticed the scrawny, grey, matted cuddly toy. Before Top Dog had woken fully, Hamish saw that the toy was a unicorn. He snuggled even closer.

His Big Folk tried to pull him away, but Hamish remained absolutely still and whined. The Big Folk bent down to stroke Top Dog and noticed the cuddly toy:

"Hey, boy. We used to have a pup called Lucky who had a toy just like this."

Top Dog grunted wearily.

Hamish's Big Folk scratched behind Top Dog's unbitten ear, and spotted an unusual marking.

"He had a marking just like this behind his left ear too," they said to each other. "Surely it can't be Lucky? Not after all this time!"

Top Dog's tail wagged limply. Was he still dreaming? he wondered, because this was the unmistakable touch, smell and voice of the Big Folk he had lost so long ago.

Hamish nudged his Big Folk in the back of their legs.

"Whoa, Hamish. What is it?"

The Big Folk looked at each other, at Hamish, then at Top Dog.

"This *is* Lucky, isn't it?"

They smiled and nodded together.

"Come on then. Time to come home, boy. Let's get you cleaned up," they said kindly to Top Dog.

Hamish jumped up and down in excitement. As he'd just won *Pet Idol,* everyone was in the mood for good things to happen. He ran around his Big Folk until his lead tangled their legs together. Top Dog looked up at the Big Folk, then looked at Hamish, who winked, and said encouragingly:

"Come on, follow me! We've got a big garden and loads of treats and toys."

Top Dog followed Hamish, feeling a mixture of relief and joy. Suddenly he turned from Hamish and his Big Folk and limped back to the wheelie bin. Seconds later, he emerged with his scrawny, grey, matted, cuddly unicorn in his jaws. Hamish wagged his tail and his Big Folk smiled. Then they headed home together.

The next morning, at about half past elevenses, Badger s-t-r-e-t-c-h-e-d in his garden, feeling very pleased with himself. He had managed to fly another batch of next door's well-buttered toast directly into his

bowl without being spotted.

As Badger the Mystical Mutt laid his head on the grass, ready for another busy day of spell practice, he thought: What a Badgical Magical job well done!

Months later, Top Dog and Hamish sat silhouetted against the winter sky in the dim light of the new moon. Looking out from their kennel, where they liked to chat, Hamish told Top Dog all about his adventures with Badger: the secret sundial, the Wim-Wim for a wowser to wind the weather up on a wet day, Nippy Nimbus, Baby Unicorn and the Crystal Cave.

Back in Badger's garden, under the light of the same new moon, Badger was enjoying a midnight feast: a higgledy-piggledy tower of toast glistening with butter.

All was well.

Down the lane, Top Dog and Hamish

looked up at the sky. Hamish turned to him and said: “Look at the stars. Aren’t they glittering and sparkly?”

“Oh yes,” agreed Top Dog. “Maybe they’re badgical magical stars. I used to wish upon them all the time. I wished I could have a home as good as this one. You know, Hamish, before I became Top Dog, I was called Lucky, and now I’m starting to believe that I definitely am. Thank you.”

ALSO PUBLISHED BY THE LUNICORN PRESS

Badger the Mystical Mutt and the Barking Boogie

ISBN: 978-0-9560640-1-4

Badger the Mystical Mutt and the Crumpled Capers

ISBN: 978-0-9569640-2-1

www.badgerthemysticalmutt.com